DISNEY
PRINCESS

5-Minute Princess Stories

DISNEY PRESS

Los Angeles • New York

Contents

A Path to the Sea

Moana loved the ocean. She loved swimming, canoeing, and walking along the shore. When Moana was old enough, Gramma Tala taught her how to surf, and Moana spent a lot of time trying to ride the waves.

After paddling into the ocean, she would float on her board and wait. Then, when the right wave came along, she would pop up and stand on her surfboard.

One day, as Moana and Pua waited for a wave, a sea turtle paddled toward them.

He swam directly up to Moana and looked right at her. She watched as he floated beside her. "Hello," she said.

There was something familiar about the sea turtle, but Moana couldn't figure out where or when she had met him before. It was almost as if she'd known him when she was a little girl.

The sea turtle stayed with Moana and Pua, playing with them in the water all day long. When Moana surfed, the turtle seemed to do the same beside her—even letting Pua stand on his back.

"You like to surf, too," Moana said, smiling at the sea turtle. She thought for a moment. "I will call you Lolo."

For many days, whenever Moana and Pua went to the ocean, Lolo found them.

They had fun swimming . . .

surfing, and playing in the waves.

One day, Moana stayed on the shore until dark to watch the ocean sparkle with moonlight.

"I knew I would find you here," said Gramma Tala, joining Moana on the beach.

The two walked under the stars, picking up seashells along the way, until Moana noticed Lolo swimming toward the shore.

They watched as the sea turtle crawled up onto the sand and over toward the coconut trees. There, Lolo started digging a hole.

"Does he need help?" Moana asked.

Gramma Tala shook her head, and the two continued to watch quietly until Lolo covered the hole and went back into the water.

"What was he doing, Gramma?" asked Moana.

"*She*, you mean," Gramma Tala said with a laugh.

Moana gasped in surprise!

"Your turtle friend just laid her eggs in the hole she dug," Gramma Tala said. "Generations of sea turtles lay their eggs right there." She told Moana how the baby turtles made their way to the ocean after hatching. "And when the females grow up, they come back to lay their eggs," she added.

"How do they remember that spot?" Moana asked. "And how do the babies even know to go to the ocean?"

"They just know," said Gramma Tala.

Moana understood. "They listen to their hearts," she said.

"That's right," Gramma Tala said proudly.

Moana checked the nesting grounds every day.

She wondered when the baby turtles would hatch and hoped she would get to see them.

One day, Moana and Pua were surfing when the sky
turned gray.

They quickly paddled to shore, and as the rain poured
down, they raced back to the village.

When they got home, they watched the trees bend
and sway as they listened to the music of the raindrops.

Soon after the storm was over, the sun came out. Moana grabbed her surfboard and hurried back to the ocean. When she got there, she couldn't believe her eyes: the storm had knocked a coconut tree right on top of the nesting grounds! Luckily, the eggs were safely buried deep underground. *But what if the baby sea turtles hatch?* she wondered. *They could be trapped!* Moana had to do something fast.

She ran back to the village and told her friends what had happened. "The eggs will hatch any day," she explained.

Her friends agreed to help, and Moana led them to the site.

They all worked together to carefully clear the fallen tree.

But then, suddenly, they heard a loud *crack*! Another palm tree had
been damaged in the storm, and it was about to fall onto the site.

"Hurry!" urged Moana. "Let's push it away from the nest."
Everyone gathered around the broken tree. They used all their
strength to push until it finally snapped and fell. "We did it!" cheered
Moana, breathing a sigh of relief.

The next day, Moana and Gramma Tala were dancing with the ocean waves when Moana saw something move in the nesting grounds.

"Gramma, look!" she said excitedly.

Lolo's eggs were hatching!

They watched as the baby sea turtles made their way out of the nest.
When a seabird swooped in and tried to capture one of the baby
turtles, Moana waved her arms and Pua chased the bird away. Moana
and her friends protected the newborns, determined to see that each
and every one made it safely to the water.

Later that day, when Moana and Pua went surfing, Lolo and her little sea turtles swam around them, paddling and playing together.

Moana smiled. She felt great knowing that she had helped Lolo's sea turtles. And there was no better way to celebrate than by enjoying the ocean together.

Belle's Flight

Belle and her father, Maurice, were on their way to Paris to visit the French National Library.

Belle couldn't wait to explore all the books. Maurice chuckled. "All of them? I hope we'll have enough time!"

But the journey would take a couple of days, so they planned to make stops along the way to sightsee.

After a few hours the first day, the travelers reached the country inn where they would spend the night.

"*Et voilà!* Cheese and warm baguettes," the landlady announced when all her guests were settled.

Maurice happily thanked her for her hospitality, but Belle's attention was caught by a young woman who was busy writing in a notebook.

What is she writing? Belle wondered. *Maybe an adventure novel or a fairy tale?*

And then came the perfect chance for Belle to find out! The
writer accidentally dropped some of her pages on the ground and
didn't notice.

"You dropped these," Belle
said, returning the papers
to the mysterious
writer.

"Thank you," the girl said. "I was so focused on my travel
journal that I didn't notice they'd fallen."

"A travel journal? How amazing!" Belle exclaimed. "Where have you traveled?"

The girl smiled and joined Belle and Maurice at their table.

Her name was Sophie.

"I have visited every town in France to search out wonderful inventions," she said.

Belle was amazed. "What is your next destination?" she asked.

"England! I'll show you how I'm traveling there!" Sophie said, heading for the door.

She led Belle and Maurice to a meadow, where she was keeping an extraordinary vehicle: a hot-air balloon!

Belle and Maurice wanted to know everything about the balloon, so Sophie showed them how it worked.

"I built it myself," she explained. "Why don't you join me for a short flight?"

Belle and Maurice were thrilled!

They scrambled into the basket and took off with Sophie on their first
balloon flight!

The world seemed so small from up high.

"The clouds are moving in fast," Sophie pointed out as they flew higher.

"Uh-oh, I think a storm is on the way!" Maurice exclaimed.

Large raindrops soon followed.

"I've never flown in a storm!" Sophie called.

"We better land!" Belle shouted over the wind.

Belle and Maurice held on tightly while Sophie turned the fire down to start the descent.

But as the balloon lowered to the ground, a gust of wind pushed it
toward a tree.

A branch sliced open the canvas! *Whoosh!*

27

The balloon plummeted to the ground! Sophie was upset that her hot-air balloon was ruined.

"Don't worry, together we can fix it!" Belle reassured her.

When the skies cleared, Belle, Maurice, and Sophie got to work. They sewed, weaved, and hammered. Soon the balloon was as good as new!

"You saved the day!" Sophie said.

As thanks, she gave Belle and Maurice a special gift:
the blueprints for her contraption.

"When we go home, we can build a balloon together!"
Belle told her father.

"But first, let me take you to Paris!" Sophie exclaimed.

Soon Philippe and his wagon were back on the road to Paris—but this time with special flying guides!

"We're nearly there!" Belle called from the balloon.

When they finally entered the French National Library, Belle
couldn't believe her eyes. There were books on every subject!

She couldn't wait to start reading! First on her list . . . travel
journals! Then books on flying! Then maps of the world, then . . .
anything and everything!

The Winter Journey

At autumn's end, the wind blew colder and the last leaves fell from the trees. The crops were harvested, and the feasting was over.

For Pocahontas and her village, the time had come to travel to their winter camp.

Pocahontas loved her home by the river, but she always looked forward to this trip. The journey meant new adventures and new places to explore. Best of all, many different villages from the Powhatan nation gathered at the winter camp to work together during the cold months.

As they walked, Pocahontas stepped off the trail and bent down
to examine the cold ground. She saw fresh tracks from an opossum, a
family of deer, and even a bobcat. Some animals were still out and about
in the winter!

Moments later, snow began to fall! Pocahontas tipped her head back,
enjoying the feeling of snow on her face.

"We are close!" called Pocahontas's father, the chief of the Powhatan.

Pocahontas's village was the first to arrive at the campsite. They hurried to unpack and set up their winter home.

Some villagers made shelters by tying woven mats onto wooden frames. Others started fires for cooking and warmth. A group of hunters prepared to find food for that night's dinner.

Pocahontas and some others set out to gather firewood. "Bring back as much dry wood as you can before dark," Pocahontas said.

Pocahontas strayed farther from the camp to search for wood. She loved the quiet of the winter forest and the soft sound of the wind. . . .

Wait, she thought. *What was that noise?*

Pocahontas put down her firewood and listened carefully. There it was again! It sounded like crying!

She climbed the nearest tree but couldn't see anything at first. Then she looked down and gasped.

A little lost deer was wandering alone in the woods. He was too young to survive on his own and needed to get back to his mother quickly.

Pocahontas climbed down from the tree. Her moccasins crunched softly in the snow. The fawn looked up and froze.

Pocahontas held her hand out. "It's all right, little one," she said. "I'm here to help."

Slowly, Pocahontas reached into her pouch and pulled out some berries. She held them flat on her palm so the breeze would carry their scent to the fawn.

The little deer prickcd up his ears with interest, and Pocahontas gently tossed the berries to him.

While the fawn happily ate his snack, Pocahontas crept around
him until she could see his tracks in the snow. She had to take the
fawn back the way he had come.

She dropped a berry on his path.
Following the tracks a little
farther, she dropped more
berries, and the fawn went
hurrying after her.

Soon they came to the bank of a creek. Scanning the icy mud at the water's edge, Pocahontas saw two sets of tracks. One belonged to the fawn, and the other, she thought, must belong to his mother.

The mother's tracks continued on the opposite bank. Pocahontas lightly ran across a path of rocks in the creek. Then she put a berry down on the far bank.

The fawn walked closer and reached out a hoof, then pulled back. He was afraid of the rushing water!

Patiently, Pocahontas piled more and more berries on the bank. The fawn gazed at the berries hungrily.

Finally, he charged right into the shallow creek. *Splash!* In a few bounds, he was across and sloshing onto the bank.

Dripping icy water, he looked up at Pocahontas and shook himself happily!

Pocahontas and the fawn followed the mother's trail to the edge of a clearing. Peering ahead, Pocahontas saw a doe pacing back and forth.

"Is that—" she started to ask.

But the fawn was already galloping across the clearing to his mother. The family was together again! Pocahontas watched, smiling and peaceful.

A branch snapped behind her. Pocahontas whirled around.

"There you are!" Pocahontas's best friend, Nakoma, called to her. "You've been gone awhile, so I came looking for you!"

"Look," Pocahontas said, pointing. "The little one was lost."

"How sweet," Nakoma said. "But we should get back. It's almost dark."

Pocahontas brightened. "Has anyone else arrived?"

"Three more villages. Probably more by now," replied Nakoma.

Pocahontas nodded. "That's the beauty of winter . . .

". . . it brings us together!"

Back at the camp, people from many different Powhatan villages were gathered. Everyone seemed to be talking at once. There was so much to catch up on, so many stories to tell!

Pocahontas snuggled under a blanket by the fire and listened. She was happy to be surrounded by the love and laughter of her family.

Seasons changed, and camps moved. But no matter where she rested her head, the land—and the families Pocahontas found there— always felt like home.

Ariel Makes Waves

One beautiful morning, Ariel, her sisters, and their father were eating breakfast under the sea.

During their meal, King Triton told the girls he had to attend to the business of ruling Atlantica and couldn't spend the day with them.

Ariel's favorite days were the ones when her father joined them on the reef, so she was particularly disappointed.

But her sisters had a plan for the day! They were going to play Ride the Current at the reef.

Once they got there, the girls counted, "One . . . two . . . three!" and flung themselves into the rushing water. Ariel, Aquata, and Andrina swam back into the current after an exciting ride, but something didn't feel right.

As they tried to move toward slower water, they realized they were stuck! They swam harder and faster, but the current was holding them in place. They were caught, and the waves were pushing them farther and farther from their home.

To make matters worse, the strong current kicked up mud from the seafloor, making it impossible for them to see anything! Far from home and unable to spot the route back, the girls were lost at sea.

"How are we going to get home?" Andrina wondered aloud.

Fortunately, Ariel had an idea: if they swam up to the surface, they could look for the reef.

"We're not supposed to go there!" Aquata warned.

But Ariel knew it was the only choice, so she grabbed her sisters' hands and swam to the surface.

"Ariel! Where are you going now?" Andrina asked when Ariel started swimming toward some rocks.

"If we head over there, maybe we can get some rest before we search for home," she responded.

But when they got to the rocks, they found a bird. "Eek! Humans!" it screeched.

"We're not going to hurt you!" Ariel assured it. "We're just mermaids and we're lost and we can't find our way back."

"Mermaids?" the bird said, fascinated. "I haven't seen mermaids in years."

"Wait! You've seen mermaids before?" Aquata asked. "Do you remember where?"

"It was in a little cove that way," the bird said, pointing with its small wing.

"Then we need to go that way to get home!" Ariel declared, turning to her sisters.

"I know who can help!" the bird said, then flapped away. Moments later, it was back . . . with dolphins. "These fellows will pull you for a while."

"Oh, thank you!" Ariel said.

"I hope you get home soon!" the bird called as it flapped out of sight again.

The girls held tight to the fins on the dolphins' backs while the dolphins skipped along the water and splashed through the waves.

When they got closer to the cove, the sisters thanked the dolphins for the lift and dove back into the water, hoping to see something familiar.

But instead two hulking shapes came into view. Sharks! The girls froze.

"Hide!" Ariel whispered. "We have to hide." Ariel and her sisters headed for the first hiding place they saw: a shipwreck.

They stopped just inside, clutching the edges of the opening and peeking at the sharks outside. Fortunately, the sharks started swimming farther away.

"Maybe we should stay here awhile . . . just to be safe," Andrina said softly. "Or at least *safer.*"

When the girls felt safe enough to talk above a whisper, Aquata breathed a sigh of relief. "Can you imagine Attina's face when we tell her about this?"

But Ariel wasn't paying attention anymore—she was exploring the ship. "Ariel!" Andrina said. "What are you doing? That's *human* stuff!"

"It's wonderful!" Ariel told her sisters. She couldn't get enough of it.

Ariel wanted to find more, but she heard someone in the distance. *"Ariel! Aquata! Andrina!"*

"What was that?" Ariel said.

Aquata's and Andrina's eyes widened, and they all quickly swam out of the shipwreck.

Outside they found two of King Triton's guards, whom the king had sent to search for them when he heard they were missing.

"We came straightaway," one of the guards said. They were impressed by the young princesses; they had nearly made it home all by themselves! But another current was on its way, and they had to fight to swim through it.

Ariel had the idea to swim down so they wouldn't get carried so far away.

"We're right behind you!" said one of the guards.

Ariel dove deeper into the blackness and eventually felt the pull of the wave lessen. Her plan had worked!

But when she looked around, no one was with her. She was alone and lost in the darkness.

"Hello? I'm lost. I need help. Can anyone hear me?" she shouted. "I can't even see anything. If only some fish could light up and show me the way . . ." she continued, talking to herself.

Just then, two little lights came on, inches from her nose. It was a fish!

"Can you help me? I'm looking for my two sisters and two guards," Ariel said. But the fish didn't answer. "Well, you don't talk, I guess. But if you've seen them, could I follow you, please?"

The fish led her through tunnels until they came across a school of fish, all with lights! They lit a path for Ariel to follow, and she eventually found her way back to the guards and her sisters.

After Ariel found them, the guards led the girls straight to the palace to see King Triton and their other sisters.

"I'm overjoyed you've returned safely," he said, "but disappointed you wandered off. You could have been lost for good!"

"Your Majesty . . ." one of the guards said, "it's worth noting that when we found the young princesses, they were well on their way home all by themselves. Quite resourceful, I think, too."

"And we didn't wander off," Aquata added. "There was a rogue wave over the reef."

"Well," King Triton said, turning to his daughters, "I am proud that you can take care of yourselves. What would you like as a reward?"

The girls thought about it, and Ariel finally spoke up. "After breakfast tomorrow, will you come play with us on the reef?"

King Triton laughed. "There is nothing I'd like more."

DISNEY PRINCESS

A Proper Princess

Princess Jasmine felt as though every day was like the one before. Her time was spent inside the palace or out in the royal gardens with her only friend, Rajah. Jasmine often wondered what life was like beyond the palace walls.

One day, Jasmine saw Jafar take a bunch of envelopes from her father.

"Who are those letters from?" she asked.

Jafar stepped forward. "Silly complaints from the people," he said. "Pure nonsense."

"*Nonsense,*" squawked Iago.

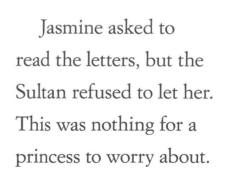

Jasmine asked to read the letters, but the Sultan refused to let her. This was nothing for a princess to worry about.

"But, Father, I want to help," said Jasmine. "I want to do *something.*"

"Your job is to be a
proper princess," he said, ushering
her out to the garden. "Just enjoy it." He smiled and
headed back to work.

Rajah followed Jasmine as she paced.

"'A proper princess'?" she repeated. "A proper princess should
have responsibilities!"

Rajah tried to comfort her. First he nuzzled his head against her arm. But that didn't seem to help.

Then Rajah let out a low growl. But Jasmine still didn't notice him.

Finally, Rajah planted himself right in front of her. That's when Jasmine noticed something in his mouth. It was one of the letters!

Jasmine hurriedly read it. The letter was from a merchant who was upset about the old town square. He said it was falling apart.

She had to find out more. But how?

Jasmine would have to see over the palace wall.
She tried . . . and tried . . . and tried . . . but it was
a very high wall! She walked around, searching for
another way.

"Rajah, I have an idea," she said, unwrapping
the long scarf from around her shoulders.

Jasmine tossed the scarf over a tree branch. Then Rajah held one end in his mouth while she held on to the other. Slowly, Rajah pulled and Jasmine rose up to the branches of the tree! She kept climbing until she could see over the wall.

And there was the old town square. Jasmine saw that it *was* in need of repair, so she quickly thought of a plan.

Jasmine rushed to tell her father about it. But he interrupted her and became angry when he learned she had climbed a tree.

"This is not proper behavior," he scolded.

Jasmine wouldn't give up. "Most of those letters are surely about the square," she said, picking up another one from his desk. "Father, have you read any of them?"

The Sultan shook his head.

Jasmine described what she'd seen and told him about her idea. "What Agrabah really needs is a new marketplace."

"With what funds?" Jafar hissed as he slithered through the doorway.

Jasmine knew in her heart that Jafar did not care about the people. "I will fund it," she said boldly. "I will happily offer my jewels for such an important project."

Jafar chuckled. "Proper princesses do not give up their jewels."

The Sultan quieted Jafar. "A central marketplace in Agrabah," he said, looking at his daughter with pride. "Yes!"

From then on, the Sultan gave Jasmine the responsibility of reading the letters. But she also had many thank-you letters to read. The merchants were so happy to see their marketplace repaired and now filled with treasures from around the world.

Jasmine was happy to see it, too.

Climbing the tree to watch the marketplace in action always made her feel closer to her people. But most of all, she finally felt like a proper princess.

The Beauty of Mistakes

Every morning, Rapunzel leaped out of bed with a huge smile on her face. Castle life was still very new to her, but she couldn't wait for the adventures each day would bring.

She loved starting her days having breakfast with her parents, King Frederic and Queen Arianna. She was fascinated by their lives and their royal duties.

One day, Rapunzel told Pascal with pride, "My parents do *so* much! I think I should do something to help . . . but what?"

She saw a broom in the corner. "I know!" she said. "I can help by doing chores around the castle, like I did in the tower."

"Princess!" gasped a housemaid. "Please stop! I'll do that!"

So Rapunzel tried to do laundry instead. But each time she tried to help, she was told, "Princess, *I* will do that!"

Rapunzel didn't understand what she was doing wrong. In the tower, she had taken care of everything.

But the things she had done well in the tower seemed like mistakes in the castle.

Rapunzel sought out the governess for advice.

"I don't think I know how to be a princess," she said, sighing. "What does a princess even do?"

"A princess makes her parents and kingdom proud," the governess replied. "And she shows that she cares about her people." She patted Rapunzel on the arm and added, "It's brave to keep trying! I'm off to run some errands, but I'll be back soon, and we can talk more then."

After the governess left, Rapunzel told Pascal, "Painting is my passion. Maybe I can make my parents proud by painting them a mural of my favorite things about Corona! Well, my favorite things so far . . ."

She found an empty wall, gathered her supplies, and began to paint.

"Pardon me, Princess, but you must stop!" the governess said when she returned. "This wall is to be covered with a map of Corona."

"I'm so sorry!" Rapunzel said. "I wanted to surprise my parents with a mural, but I messed this up, too!"

"There, there," the governess comforted her. "It takes time to learn all the responsibilities of being a princess. The important thing is that you keep trying."

The governess looked at the painted scene on the wall and said, "This really is quite lovely. I could never paint half as well as you do!"

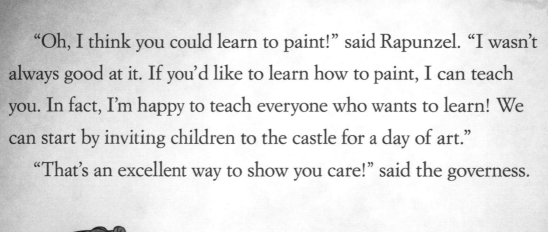

"Oh, I think you could learn to paint!" said Rapunzel. "I wasn't always good at it. If you'd like to learn how to paint, I can teach you. In fact, I'm happy to teach everyone who wants to learn! We can start by inviting children to the castle for a day of art."

"That's an excellent way to show you care!" said the governess.

On the day of the art lesson, there wasn't a cloud in the sky. Rapunzel, Eugene, and the castle staff set up easels with large sheets of paper all over the courtyard.

"What shall we paint, Princess Rapunzel?" asked one girl.

"Whatever you see or imagine," said Rapunzel. Then she tapped her heart and added, "Or whatever you feel."

Rapunzel strolled through the courtyard, stopping at each easel and encouraging each young artist.

"It was supposed to be a bird," sighed one boy, "but I made a lot of mistakes. I'm just not a good painter."

Rapunzel said, "I know what it's like to feel discouraged. You're trying something new, so it might feel frustrating. But trust yourself and keep trying!"

She pointed to the colorful painting and smiled. "Personally, I think you've created a very special, one-of-a-kind bird!"

The boy beamed and said, "Thank you, Princess Rapunzel!"

He dipped his paintbrush in some blue paint and kept working.

Seemingly out of nowhere, dark clouds filled the sky. Eugene said, "Uh, Rapunzel, I don't want to rain on your parade, but it looks like—"

The rumble of thunder cut off Eugene's words. Suddenly, it began to pour!

Everyone was getting soaked, and so were all the paintings!

The castle staff helped the children dry off while Rapunzel and
Eugene hung the paintings near the fireplace to dry. Her day of art felt
like one more huge mistake.

She wondered, *What would a princess do?*

Just then, she noticed the light from the fireplace glowing through
the paintings.

"Eugene," she said, "what does this remind you of?"

"The lanterns!" he said, smiling at her.

"The rain may have cut our painting lesson short, but we can still have our day of art right here!" Rapunzel announced.

The children gathered around as she explained her plan.

"We're going to take these dried paintings and make them into lanterns!" Rapunzel said. "Very special, one-of-a-kind lanterns!"

Soon everyone was having fun turning their paintings into small, colorful lanterns.

Later, Queen Arianna and King Frederic entered the room.

"Mom! Dad! I've had the most amazing day!" Rapunzel said brightly. "Things didn't go as planned. But maybe what I've been thinking of as mistakes aren't mistakes. They're just me being me, learning and trying as I go along. And they're all steps to something beautiful, just like the lanterns we made today."

"You're learning and trying in your own unique way," said Queen Arianna. "And that's what makes you a very special, one-of-a-kind princess!"

The Dragon Boat Race

The Duanwu Festival was quickly approaching. The celebration took place in China every spring, on the fifth day of the fifth lunar month. Mulan's favorite part was the dragon boat race. Each spring, Mulan watched the boats from other villages race down the river.

This year, Mulan wanted to do more than watch.

"Our village should enter the race!" Mulan told her family.

Her father agreed this would bring honor to their village, but her mother was worried. The village had never taken part before. Would they know what to do?

Grandma Fa reminded them that Mulan had once never traveled beyond their village. "There's a first time for everything."

Mulan announced her idea to the village.

The villagers were hesitant but excited to try something new.

Mulan explained that they would learn, just as the teams from other villages had learned.

"There's a first time for everything," she said.

Outside the temple of the ancestors, Mulan asked Mushu to help choose what colors to paint the boat.

"It should look like me, of course!" Mushu said.

Together, Mulan and her teammates painted the boat to match Mushu's fiery red scales and orange belly.

Mushu admired their handiwork. "It does sort of look like me," Mushu said, "if not quite as handsome."

Practice began the next day. Mushu volunteered to be the drummer. "I've had a lot of practice from banging a gong all these years."

Mulan showed Mushu how to keep a steady rhythm for the team to follow. She clapped her hands. One, two, three. Mushu thumped the drum. The villagers arced their paddles through the air to the beat. Soon they were paddling in unison.

Mulan joined the team. As the sweep, it was her job to steer with a
long oar.

They pushed out into the water. At first the boat zigged and zagged,
but then the villagers heard Mushu's steady *wham, wham, wham.*

They followed the beat and glided through the water.

Finally, it was the day of the race. Mulan and her team lined up their boat with the others, excited and eager for the race.

When the race began,
the dragon boats zoomed off.
Each drummer pounded out a different rhythm.

As the other boats whizzed past, Mulan's team struggled to hear
Mushu's steady beat.

Mulan tried to steer as the waves from the other teams slapped against the sides of their boat. She clutched her oar fearfully as the boat tipped this way and that. The drum bounced out of Mushu's hands and into the water. He reached out to grab it and fell in! *Splash!*

Mulan helped her teammates fish Mushu out of the river. He raced back to his spot. But the team didn't notice their boat heading for the reeds. They crashed!

The villagers slumped in their seats. How could they finish the race now?

"We can't give up!" Mulan told her team. She knew quitting would not bring honor to their village. They'd lost their drum, but they still had their paddles, their boat, and their team.

"It's true we've never paddled without a drum," Mulan said. "But there's a first time for everything. And there's one thing we can do that isn't a first . . . work together."

Mulan reminded the villagers that together they'd built and painted a dragon boat.

Together they'd trained for the race.

"Together we can get to the finish line!" she cheered.

"And I can still give you a steady beat!" Mushu said. He clapped his hands.

The villagers smiled and lined up their paddles, ready to row.

Together, Mulan and her teammates steered the boat back onto the river. The villagers pushed their paddles through the water to Mushu's beat, again and again, until they reached the finish line.

The crowd onshore greeted Mulan's team with cheers.

Although they were the last dragon boat to arrive, they were the first to complete the race without a drum.

That night, Mulan, her teammates, and the rest of the village found another thing they could do together . . . celebrate!

Aurora Plays the Part

Briar Rose dreamed a lot. Most often, she dreamed of meeting someone new, someone her age, someone she could talk to. But her aunts had set boundaries on how far she was allowed to wander, so her dream never came true.

One day, she found a bunny struggling in a shallow stream. His family hadn't noticed he'd fallen, so Rose dropped her basket and ran to help.

Rose quickly caught up to the bunny's family and lowered him gently to the grass. When she stood up, she realized she was somewhere she'd never been before.

Then a splash in the stream startled her. She went to see what kind of animal was headed her way. But it wasn't an animal at all—it was a girl.

"Hello," Rose hesitantly called to the girl.

"Hi," the girl responded. "I'm Grace."

Grace explained that she and her grandmother were part of a traveling acting troupe, and their caravan had broken down nearby.

The girls got to talking and soon felt as if they'd known each other forever. Rose was sad to leave later that afternoon, but she knew she had to get home.

When she arrived, she told her aunts all about her day. "We set those boundaries for a reason," Aunt Flora reminded her, "to keep you safe."

"I know, but what about Grace?" Rose asked. "It sounds like she and her troupe may need help."

The aunts assured Rose they would go help Grace and her troupe. They instructed Rose to stay at home.

But she quietly followed her aunts through the forest. They were upset when they saw her, but agreed to let her come along with them . . . just that once.

Rose soon felt a tap on her shoulder. It was Grace! "Rose! You're here! You have to come meet my grandmother," Grace said, tugging on Rose's sleeve.

"Call me Madam Talia," the woman said when they found her. "You must be the girl Grace met in the forest."

"Yes, hello." Rose was fascinated by all that surrounded her. "So, you put on plays? Where? Who makes these costumes? I think I'd love to perform on a stage."

But not all her questions got answered. It wasn't long before the aunts came into the tent and told her it was time to go home.

"Flora and I are going to help them find the parts they need to repair their wagons. The journey will take us three days," Aunt Fauna said.

"We'll escort you back to the cottage first though," Aunt Flora said to Rose.

"Can I come along?" Grace asked. "I should get more water anyway."

"Of course," Aunt Merryweather said, turning to Madam Talia, "as long as it's all right with your grandmother."

"Have fun, girls!" Madam Talia said.

On the walk back home, Rose and Grace stayed a few paces behind the aunts.

"It must be so nice to have a home," Grace said.

"It must be so nice to always see someplace new," Rose responded.

"It's too bad we can't switch places," Grace said with a sigh.

"Then *I* would get some adventure, and *you* would have one place to call home," Rose said longingly.

The girls thought about it . . . and quickly agreed to try to switch places!

Grace—wearing Rose's clothes—headed straight to the cottage. The next morning, she excused herself and joined Rose back at the troupe's camp, where Rose had stayed the night undetected.

After switching back into their regular clothes, the girls told Madam Talia that Rose's aunt had given Rose permission to watch the rehearsals.

"I'm happy you've returned," Madam Talia said, beaming at her. "Would you like to have a role in the play?"

"I'd love to!" Rose said.

"Welcome to the Errant Band of Actors!" Madam Talia cried.

Rose learned her lines, ate lunch with the troupe, and had a great time.

But soon the sunlight began to fade, and the girls had to say their good-byes for the night. They switched clothes once again for night two of their plan.

When Rose woke up the next morning, she was surprised to find that Grace wasn't back yet. As her nerves bundled tighter and tighter, Rose walked across the campsite toward Madam Talia.

"Rose!" Madam Talia greeted her. "Why are you wearing Grace's clothes?"

Rose gulped. "I have a confession." The story of Rose and Grace's switch tumbled out.

Madam Talia quickly gathered the troupe to look for Grace.

Fortunately, they found her hidden in Rose's hide-and-seek tree. Rose had told Grace about it during one of her stories.

"On my way back this morning, I spotted some strangers by the stream," Grace explained. "I hid and was too scared to leave."

Madam Talia scowled at Rose and Grace. "I don't need to tell you what a foolish scheme this was."

"I just wanted to experience some of the outside world, to be around other people," Rose said.

"And I just wanted to know what a real home felt like," said Grace.

"I'm sorry," they said in unison.

On their walk back to the campsite, they ran into Aunt Flora, Aunt Fauna, and Aunt Merryweather. Madam Talia filled them in on what Grace and Rose had been up to.

"I'm truly sorry," Rose said. "I just saw a chance to live a dream, and I took it."

"We want you to live your dreams," Aunt Fauna said. "But we set these rules to keep you safe."

"You'd better go say your good-byes," Aunt Flora told her.

Near Madam Talia's tent, Grace was finishing up her own conversation with her grandmother. The girls ducked into the tent to swap clothes.

"Are you in terrible trouble?" Rose asked when they were back in their own clothes.

"Meal cooking *and* cleanup duty through our next ten shows," Grace said with a groan.

"Worth it?" Rose asked.

"Worth it," Grace said, grinning.

When they emerged from the tent, they found Madam Talia smiling next to Rose's aunts.

"Rose," Aunt Flora began, "we've been speaking to Madam Talia, and we've decided—"

"To let you stay for the dress rehearsal!" Aunt Merryweather cheered.

Rose clapped her hands to her face in surprise. "Oh, my! Thank you!"

It was a night Rose would not soon forget. She'd get to be a part of something: a cast, songs, a story. And it seemed like a wonderful dream come true.

Disney PRINCESS
Tiana's Growing Experiment

Tiana sighed and hung up the phone. "I've called every pepper farmer in the state of Louisiana, and none of them have what I'm looking for," she told Naveen.

Tiana took a magazine off the counter and showed it to him. "I read about ghost peppers in this article. I wanted to try them in my jambalaya. The problem is they're from India. No one grows them here."

As Naveen went upstairs, Tiana slowly flipped through the pages of the magazine. Suddenly, something caught her eye. There, at the bottom of the credits page, was an address for one of the Indian farms the magazine writer had visited for the article.

Tiana decided to write them a letter and ask if they would be willing to sell her some seeds for the peppers!

A few weeks later, Tiana was cooking up a batch of gumbo when Naveen came into the restaurant and handed her an envelope.

As she opened it, a small packet fell to the floor. Tiana set it aside and began to read the letter aloud:

"'Dear Princess Tiana, we have heard tales of your famous food and are honored that you would like to use the ghost pepper in your cuisine. Enclosed, please find the seeds you will need to grow them.'"

Tiana couldn't wait to get started. There was just one problem. She knew how to *cook* a pepper, but she'd never *grown* anything before.

She decided to make a stop at the library to check out a few books all about gardening.

By the end of the evening, she felt ready to start her garden.

The next morning, she went to the market to buy supplies. She found pots, gloves, a trowel, and a watering can. Then she ordered dirt and fertilizer to be delivered to the restaurant.

Back at the restaurant, Tiana went up to the roof deck. She was going to turn the space into her garden!

Once everything she needed had been delivered, Tiana got started.

Each morning, before the restaurant opened, Tiana checked on her peppers.

"I hope I planted them correctly," she told Naveen one night. "What if they don't grow?"

"They will," Naveen said. "Just be patient."

Finally, one morning, she saw a spot of green! Tiana was so excited to see her peppers start to grow that she decided to try her hand at growing other things, too.

A few days later, Tiana was planting her new vegetables when she heard a familiar voice.

"Tia? Are you up here?"

Tiana looked up just as Charlotte opened the door to the roof. "What on earth are you doing? You're completely covered in dirt! It's filthy up here!"

Tiana smiled at her friend. "Welcome to my garden, Lottie. Want to help?"

"You want me to touch . . . that?" Charlotte asked. "There could be bugs in there!"

"Ah, come on, Charlotte. It's just a little dirt," Naveen said with a wink. "And Tiana's having fun. In fact, she's having so much fun, I'm thinking of trying it."

Charlotte looked over at Naveen. "You're going to get your hands all dirty? I'm getting out of here before any of that filth gets on my new dress!"

Naveen followed Charlotte back down the steps, but a few minutes later he returned with a cucumber. "Okay . . . what do I do?"

"Well, first you have to get the seeds out of it," Tiana said.

In the kitchen, she explained that the seeds would have to be washed and then dried for a few days.

"A few days?" Naveen cried. "But I wanted to work in the garden with you today!"

"What was it you told me? Be patient?" she said, smiling.

Just then, Louis came into the kitchen looking for a snack. "Did I hear someone say 'garden'?" he asked. "Can I try?"

Tiana smiled at the friendly alligator. "Of course you can," she said.

A few days later, Tiana tended to her existing plants while Naveen and Louis got busy planting their crops. But Naveen wasn't finding gardening so easy.

Fortunately, with Tiana's help, Naveen fixed his pots.

Then, day after day, the trio trooped up to the roof to check on their plants.

"Hey, look at that!" Naveen shouted.

"Look at what?" Charlotte asked. She had come up to the roof to find her friends.

"My cucumbers!" Naveen said. "I did it!"

"All that dirt really doesn't bother you?" she asked.

Naveen shrugged. "Honestly, it's kind of fun. It's messy, but look what I have to show for it."

Charlotte wandered around the roof, looking at everyone's plants. "Wow, Tia," she said, "those peppers are really getting big! And, Louis, those radishes do look tasty. You all seem to be having so much fun. Maybe getting a little dirty isn't so bad. . . ." She paused to consider.

"Okay, I'm in!" she announced a moment later. "But I want to grow something pretty, like flowers."

Tiana walked over to her friend. "Come on, Lottie. We'll go to the market and find you the perfect flowers to grow."

The next morning, Charlotte put on an old dress and covered it with the biggest apron she could find.

Tiana laughed when she saw her friend. "I think you may be a little overdressed, Lottie," she said.

Charlotte shook her head. "I said I'd touch the dirt. I didn't say I was going to let the dirt touch me! Now come on, show me what to do."

Over the next few weeks, everyone spent as much time as they could working on their plants. Even Charlotte got excited when she saw her flowers start to bloom.

"Look at that," she said. "They're so pretty."

Naveen surveyed the roof. There were pots everywhere! "What are we going to do with all these vegetables?" he asked.

Tiana smiled. "Leave it to me," she said. "Meet me back here at five o'clock on Monday night."

That Monday, the friends gathered on the roof.

Charlotte gasped as she looked around. "Tia," she said, "you turned all your vegetables into dinner!"

Tiana smiled. "I realized we had grown the perfect ingredients for a summer salad. And for anyone daring enough to try it, the first batch of my new jambalaya recipe. Guaranteed to set your mouth on fire!"

Merida's Challenge

Merida couldn't stop laughing. "You three wee bairns think you can climb the Crone's Tooth?"

The Crone's Tooth was the tallest mountain around.

"Only the biggest and bravest people have climbed it—including me," she continued. "Don't even try."

Harris, Hubert, and Hamish scowled. Of course they would give it a try! They were big and brave, too. They had to prove it to Merida.

As they stood at the foot of the towering rock, Harris and Hubert weren't so sure it was a good idea. But Hamish was ready.

"I'll show her," he said to his brothers.

They gave him a boost, but he struggled to find handholds in the slippery rock.

A little way up, the rock Hamish was standing on fell away. He was left dangling . . . by his fingertips!

Harris and Hubert hurried to fetch Merida.

They found her in the castle and told her what had happened to Hamish at the Crone's Tooth.

"Och, no!" cried Merida. "What have I done? I didn't really mean you should try to climb it yourselves! Come on, we have to get Angus."

But Merida was so worried she couldn't think straight. "Where are my arrows?" she cried to her brothers. Fortunately, Hubert was one step ahead of her, and he tossed them to his sister.

When they got to Angus in the stables, Merida was still worried they wouldn't make it to the Crone's Tooth in time to save Hamish. "I'm all thumbs," Merida said. "I'll never get this bridle on!" Harris quickly helped his sister get ready to ride.

Soon they were galloping toward the Crone's
Tooth. "Faster, Angus!" Merida urged. "Faster!"

Hamish was still hanging on when they arrived . . . but barely. He kicked the wall, trying to find a foothold. Something blue caught Merida's eye. "Wisps! I should've known." She called out to her brother, "Hold on, Hamish! Please hold on!"

Merida scanned the trees around the clearing. "Quick! Harris,
Hubert! Gather as many fallen leaves as you can. I have an idea!"
Soon they had formed a large pile under Hamish.

Merida looped a rope around her waist and knotted it tightly. She tied the end to an arrow.

Stepping back, she sent the arrow flying over the high branch of a tree.

Then Harris hurried to fetch the arrow from the ground and tied the rope to Angus's saddle.

"Angus," Merida said, "walk up that hill."

The branch groaned as Angus pulled the rope taut. Everyone held their breath.

"Keep pulling slowly," Merida said. The branch groaned again.

The rope began to hoist Merida into the air.

Fragments of rock pattered down as Hamish began to lose his grip. "Just a wee bit longer, Hamish!" yelled Merida. "Ignore those wisps!" Finally, Merida was high enough to grab her brother. "I've got you!" Merida laughed, hugging him tightly. "Angus, you can start walking backward now."

Angus slowly lowered Merida and Hamish over the pile of leaves. When she was sure it was safe, Merida dropped Hamish on the leaves. The rescue mission was a success!

"How brave you all were," Merida said to her brothers. "You, Hamish, for hanging in there so long. And you, Harris and Hubert, for being so calm and reliable all through the rescue." But the triplets had one more thought on their minds. . . .

As the wisps flew away to cause mischief elsewhere, the brothers crossed their arms and looked to their sister.

"Okay, okay!" Merida said, laughing. "I promise I won't question your bravery again!"

Snow White and the Three Giants

Since meeting the Dwarfs long before, Snow White knew the path to their cottage quite well. She often could be found visiting them.

But one day, because she was busy talking to her woodland creature friends, she took a wrong turn in the woods and got lost on her way to the Dwarfs' home.

When she found another cottage in the woods, she knocked on the door, hoping whoever lived there could help her find her way. But no one answered. She noticed that the door was slightly open, so she stepped inside and exclaimed, "Oh, my!"

Instead of a neat row of seven little chairs, she saw three enormous chairs!

As she walked
farther into the
cottage, she saw
a fire roaring and
crackling in an
enormous hearth.

Then, just as Snow
White discovered
the enormous dining
table, the ground
began to shake.

"Oh, no!" she
gasped.

With a groan, the door opened all the way, and in came three of the tallest people Snow White had ever seen! They lumbered straight toward her.

What should I do now? wondered Snow White.

Snow White cleared her throat and stepped into their view. "Excuse me," she said bravely.

The giants jumped back in surprise.

"I'm so sorry," Snow White continued quickly. "I let myself in by mistake. Let me introduce myself. My name is Snow White."

"Oh!" said the largest giant. "It's okay. You just scared us a bit. We don't get visitors here often."

"But now that you're here," said the least-big giant, "you should join us for dinner."

The three giants knelt down to introduce themselves to Snow White. She was relieved they were as kind as the Dwarfs had been when they first met her.

The least-big giant helped her climb up on his chair. "You'll need some cushions," he said, laughing.

"And here is a small plate and glass," said the middle-sized giant.

"Thank you," said Snow White. "You're all so kind!"

The next day, Snow White told the Dwarfs about her adventure.

"G-g-giants?" stammered Bashful.

Sleepy yawned. "Aren't they dangerous?"

"Not at all," Snow White reassured them.

"Don't trust them!" Grumpy said. "You can't trust anyone tall!"

"But I'm taller than you," Snow White said. "You'll just have to come and meet them."

Snow White thought for a few days about how to introduce the giants to the Dwarfs. She just knew they'd get along.

Back at the castle one night, Snow White had the perfect idea. She addressed ten party invitations and made a list of the delicious food she'd make. All she needed then was a game to get everyone laughing.

On the day of the party, Snow White announced,
"We're going to play Snap. I'll point out something
about me, and if it's true for you, shout 'SNAP!' And
then it's someone else's turn."

"Oh, I love games like this," Doc said, chuckling.

"Here we go," said Snow
White, thinking for a moment.
"I have two eyes."

"SNAP!" yelled
the giants.

"SNAP!"
yelled the
Dwarfs.

Snow White turned to Bashful, who was up next.

"Um, I have two ears," he said quietly.

"SNAP!" called the giants.

"SNAP!" called the Dwarfs.

Next it was the largest giant's
turn. "Ahem. I have one nose."

"SNAP!"
shouted the giants.

"SNAP!"
shouted the Dwarfs.

"I guess we have a lot in common after all," Grumpy admitted.

"Yes, you do!" said Snow White.
"We all have things in common! And
there's actually one more thing you have
in common . . . you are *all* my friends!"
"SNAP!" cheered the Dwarfs.
"SNAP!" cheered the giants.

Disney PRINCESS

Opening Night

It was opening night at the royal theater, and Princess Cinderella was excited to see the show. As the curtain went up, the star stepped onto the stage.

Cinderella smiled. She knew the performer. It was Carine, a singer she had met long before becoming a princess.

Years before, Cinderella's stepmother, Lady Tremaine, had hosted a gathering at her chateau where girls could learn how to play an instrument and take singing lessons.

Lessons sounded boring to Lady Tremaine's two daughters, Drizella and Anastasia, but Cinderella thought it was a wonderful idea.

"I'd love to come!" she said.

Lady Tremaine narrowed her eyes. "Why, Cinderella, do you really have that much free time?"

"Well, I just meant—"

"You have far too many chores to do," Cinderella's stepmother continued.

The next day, lessons began. Cinderella slipped away from her chores to peek in. One girl, standing off to the side, caught her attention. She had the sweetest voice Cinderella had ever heard.

Her name was Carine.

Anastasia and Drizella were immediately jealous of Carine's talent.

"You're not special," hissed Drizella. "Your voice is so quiet no one can even hear you."

"Which is a good thing, since you sound like a goose," mocked Anastasia.

Later that evening, Lady Tremaine said, "Anastasia, you must do something about your flute playing. Work harder, dear!"

"It's not my fault," replied Anastasia. "I always play the right notes, but my flute plays something else. I think it's broken."

"I see," said Lady Tremaine. "I'll have Cinderella pick up a new one for you."

But at the music shop the next morning, the shopkeeper couldn't find anything wrong with Anastasia's flute.

"Even so, Anastasia wants a new one," Cinderella explained.

The man handed Cinderella a new flute and asked what she planned to do with the old one.

"I don't think anyone will mind if I keep it," she answered. Cinderella had hoped to learn how to play the flute. She wanted to make music for her animal friends.

On her way home, Cinderella saw Carine.

"You sing beautifully," Cinderella said.

"Do you really think so?" asked Carine. "Anastasia said I sounded like a goose."

"That's not true!" Cinderella exclaimed. "Your voice is as sweet as a songbird's. I have an idea." It was time for Carine to see for herself how good she was!

First Cinderella had Carine sing for the shopkeeper at the music store. Carine, feeling a little shy, sang softly for him.

"Charming!" said the shopkeeper.

The two friends then went to the bakery. This time, Carine sang more confidently. The baker clapped, sending up clouds of flour dust!

At the perfumery, Carine's voice was strong and full of energy.

"Superb," cooed a patron. "You're so very talented."

Carine was delighted!

At the next lesson, Lady Tremaine announced that Madame LaVoix,
a famous opera singer, would be coming the next day. She'd be selecting
one student to study with her. It was the chance of a lifetime!

"I'll be right by your side for the audition," Cinderella told Carine. "Just be yourself. Remember, your voice is as sweet as a songbird's."

"Thank you," said Carine. "You know, I really do think I have a chance!"

That night, as Cinderella was practicing the flute, her stepsisters and Lady Tremaine barged into her room.

"That's my flute!" shouted Anastasia. "Give it back!"

"You have no talent," Drizella scoffed.

Lady Tremaine was furious. "You can't be trusted, Cinderella. You are forbidden from being anywhere near the salon tomorrow. I want you to be outdoors gathering firewood."

"But I've already collected enough for winter," said Cinderella.

"Then you will gather enough for two winters!"

When Carine arrived at the salon the next day, she missed Cinderella.

"You can't sing," sneered Drizella as Anastasia cackled.

When it was Carine's turn to audition for Madame LaVoix, she opened her mouth to sing, but nothing came out.

In the meantime, Cinderella's friends had been working with her since dawn to collect firewood. As soon as they finished, Cinderella ran inside, hoping to be in time for the audition.

She arrived just as Drizella and Anastasia were warbling their way through an off-key duet. It was dreadful.

Madame LaVoix headed for her carriage. She hadn't found anyone who could be her student.

Carine told Cinderella what had happened.

"It's not too late!" Cinderella said. "If you believe in yourself, you can do anything."

Carine gave Cinderella a hug. "I think I'm ready to sing now."

Cinderella called out to the opera star. "Madame LaVoix! If you please, Carine would like to sing for you," she said.

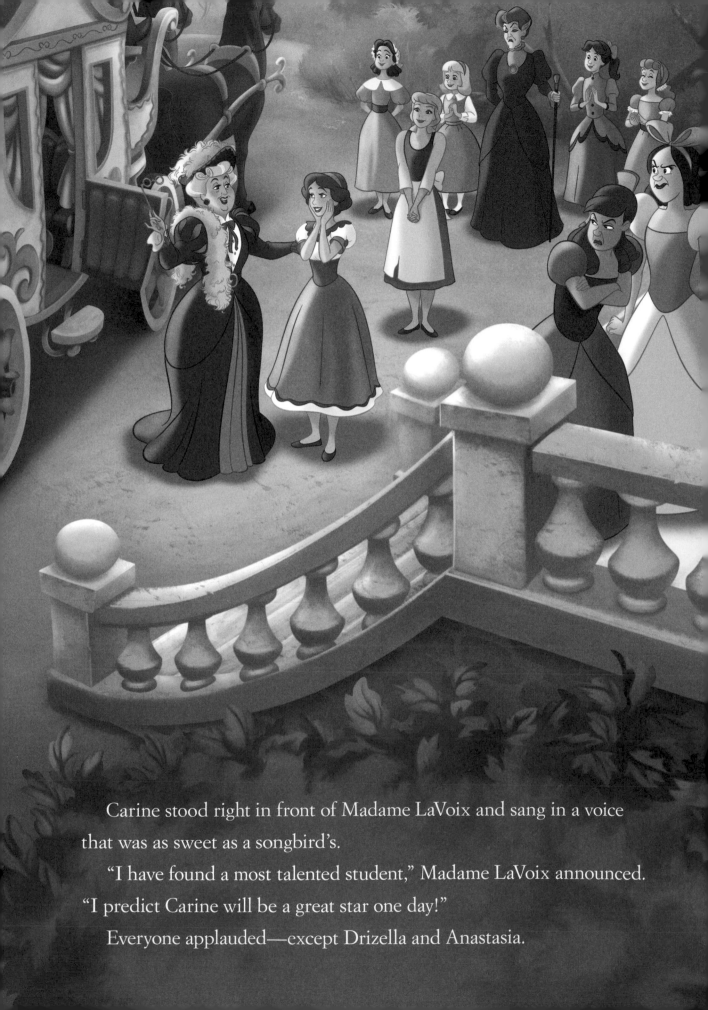

Carine stood right in front of Madame LaVoix and sang in a voice
that was as sweet as a songbird's.

"I have found a most talented student," Madame LaVoix announced.
"I predict Carine will be a great star one day!"

Everyone applauded—except Drizella and Anastasia.

That night, Gus and Jaq brought Cinderella a surprise.

"The flute!" she gasped. "Oh, thank you!"

Cinderella promised she'd practice as much as possible so she could play a song for all her friends!

Back at the theater, Princess Cinderella hugged Carine after the show. "Your voice is as sweet as ever," she said. "You had the whole audience under your spell."

"Thank you," Carine said. "I couldn't have done it without you, Princess."

Suddenly, a young performer ran up to Carine. "I did it," she said. "I sang out loud!"

"I heard you," said Carine. "Your voice was as sweet as a songbird's."

Princess Cinderella couldn't help smiling.